King Julien Jobs

Timo

Mort

King Julien

Maurice

Adapted by Benjamin Hulme-Cross

King Julien was fishing.
He had seen something
in the water and he
wanted to get it, but
there was a problem ...

Maurice had a long
list of jobs for King Julien.

The jobs needed to be done.

King Julien sighed and pulled up his fishing rod.

"Why is Mort on your
fishing line?" asked Maurice.

"I want him to get that sack in the water." said King Julien. "It says '*king*' and '*magic*'!" he cried. "Mort is going to catch it for me!"

"Watch this!" said King Julien. Mort dived towards the sack.

Wheeeeee!

"I've got it!" cried Mort.
Suddenly something snatched the sack ...
and Mort! It was a crocodile!

"Mort!" cried King Julien and Maurice, and they pulled hard on the rod. The crocodile pulled back.

Finally, they pulled Mort and the sack free.
"I'm okay!" said Mort.

"Look! Magic beans!" said King Julien, looking into the sack.

The beans were coffee beans – but King Julien did not know that. He ate some.

"No!" cried Maurice.

Uh oh!

Gasp!

Choke!

Help!

"Help!" King Julien cried. Mort butted King
Julien with his head and the beans flew out!

"What's this picture?" asked Mort.

"It must be a machine to get the magic out of the beans!" said King Julien. "I know, perhaps Timo can help make me a machine like this!"

They took the sack to Timo's lab.
"I need a special machine!" said King Julien.

So Timo made him one.

"This *should* work but it *might* explode," said Timo.

"I'm willing to take that chance," said King Julien.

Clatter

Clunk

Trickle

"I wonder what powers the drink will give me,"
cried King Julien. "Flight? Super strength?"

Timo poured the drink and King Julien snatched
the cup. He took a sip and waited.

Nothing happened so he drank the rest.

Suddenly, King Julien had gone!

The drink made King Julien super speedy.

Vroom!

"I feel *awesome!*" he cried.

He snatched up his list of jobs and ran around doing them all *very* fast!

"Everything's done!" he cried.

So he sat down to read a book.
"What about your jobs?" asked Maurice.

"They're all done!" said King Julien.

Maurice was not pleased. "You rushed!" he said. "The jobs have not been done well."

So King Julien had to do all his jobs again!